To: _____

From: _____

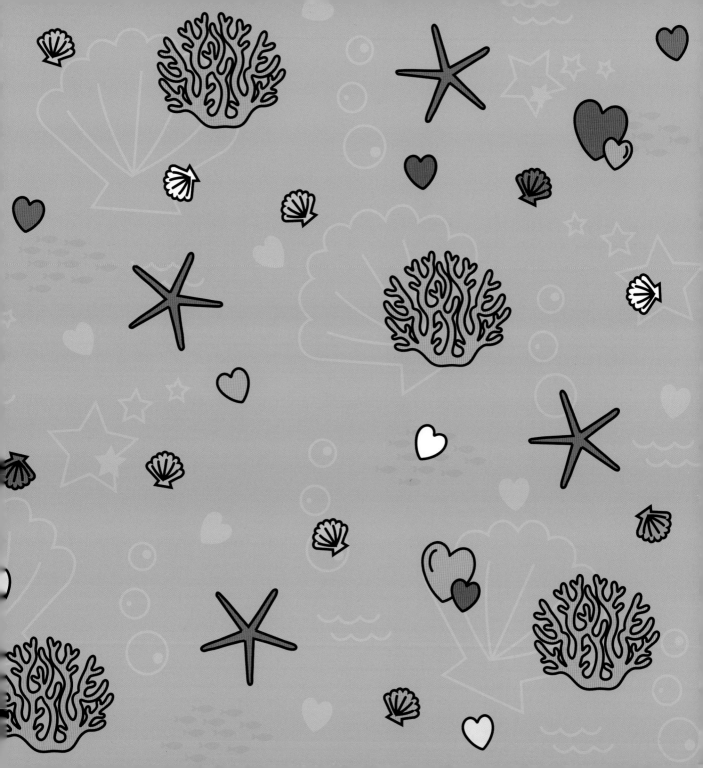

tiger tales

5 River Road, Suite 128, Wilton, CT 06897
Published in the United States 2021
Text by Danielle McLean
Text copyright © 2021 Little Tiger Press Ltd.
Images used under license from Shutterstock.com
Incidental artwork by Julie Clough
ISBN-13: 978-1-66434006-0
ISBN-10: 1-66434006-8
Printed in China • LTP/2700/3665/0920
2 4 6 8 10 9 7 5 3 1

For more insight and activities, visit us at www.tigertalesbooks.com

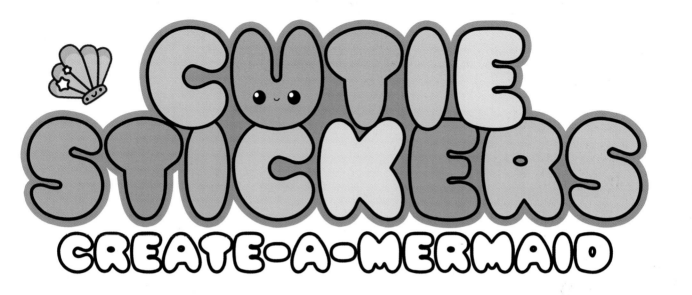

CUTIE STICKERS
CREATE-A-MERMAID

tiger tales

CUTE FRUIT

Let your imagination run wild and have a mer-mazing time! Add tails, arms, eyes, mouths, and more to make your very own mermaid sticker friends.

A DREAM COME BLUE

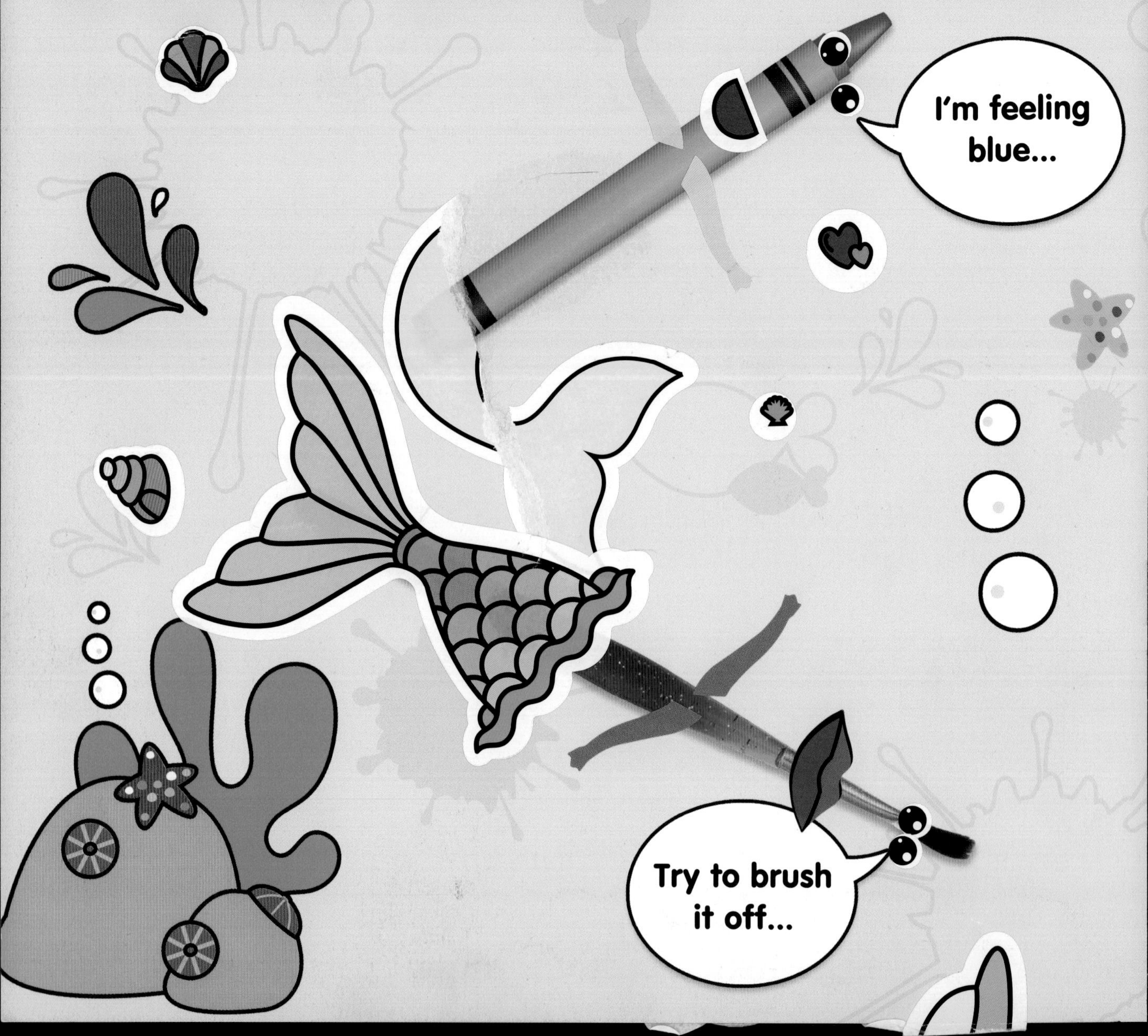

UNBE-LEAF-ABLE

FRUITY AND THE BEAST

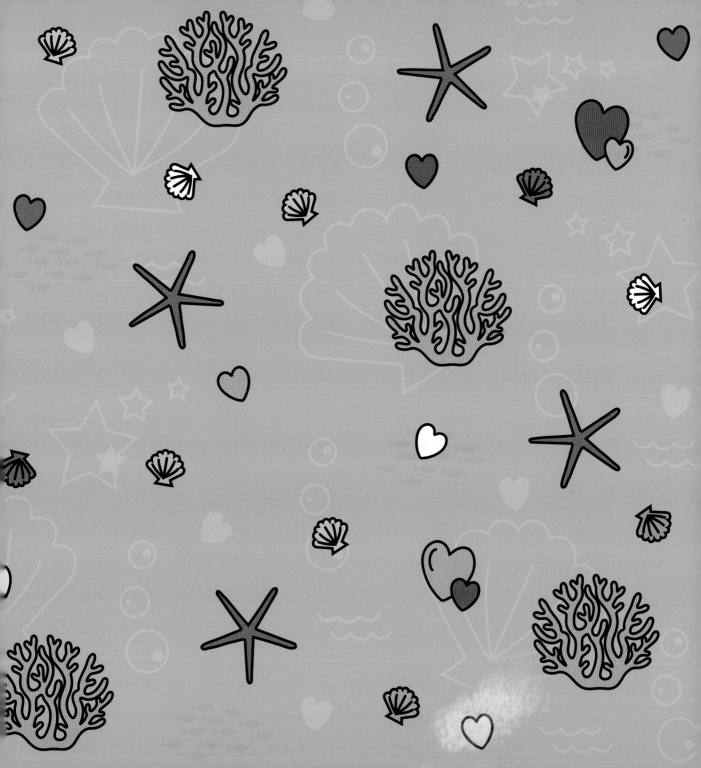

Also available: